The SECRET Woodland ACTIVITY BOOK

By Mia Underwood

Button BOOKS

There is a **secret** woodland that really exists, on a distant island in Scandinavia, which few people have ever seen. Boats sail by and don't notice it is there because it is surrounded by a magic spell. In this secret woodland, only special people can see the magic. The woodfolk that live there only become visible for the lucky few.

Draw yourself entering the woods. What might you need to take with you?

Welcome to the woods

The woodfolk would like to invite you into their secret woodland. They think that you can help them with some important jobs: solving puzzles, finding lost treasures, and making connections with hidden creatures in the woods.

Are you ready for an adventure? Then let's go!

Some of the woodfolk are a bit shy and like to hide.
How many can you spot? Add in some more creatures to
keep them company, using the stickers found in the
middle of the book.

The creatures that live in
the SECRET woodland are called

Woodfolk

Let me introduce you to a few of them.

Stardust

Pip

Pop

Lulu

Nisse

Hopper

Can you think of a good name for the ones
that are missing? Write them in the spaces.

Spot the difference

Find 10 differences between the two woodland sprites.

Can you put the woodfolk into height order by numbering them with 1 for the shortest and 7 the tallest?

Paper-fastener
crafty creatures

Make your very own woodland creature, with moveable arms and legs. You could add a stick to the back to transform it into a puppet, or attach a loop of string to hang it on your wall.

YOU WILL NEED
----
* Letter or tabloid-sized sheets of card stock
* Scissors
* Tracing paper or access to a photocopier
* Pencil and pencil sharpener
* Colored markers or pencils
* Paper (brad) fasteners, 4 per character
* Strong glue
* Adhesive putty or cork

1. Choose from the opposite page which head, body, arms, legs, wings, and tail you would like your creature to have.

2. Trace the body parts onto letter or tabloid-sized card stock (depending on how big you want to make your character). Or, photocopy the opposite page and then glue the paper onto the card stock.

3. Color the body parts in and then cut them out with scissors. Glue the head and tail onto the body and wait for them to dry.

4. Make a hole for the paper fasteners, where shown, on the body, arms, and legs. Place a piece of adhesive putty or cork on the back of the card stock where you want to make the hole and carefully push the point of a pencil through from the front to the back. Adult assistance might be required for this part. Push a paper fastener through the holes to join the arms and legs onto the body, securing at the back by folding out the pins.

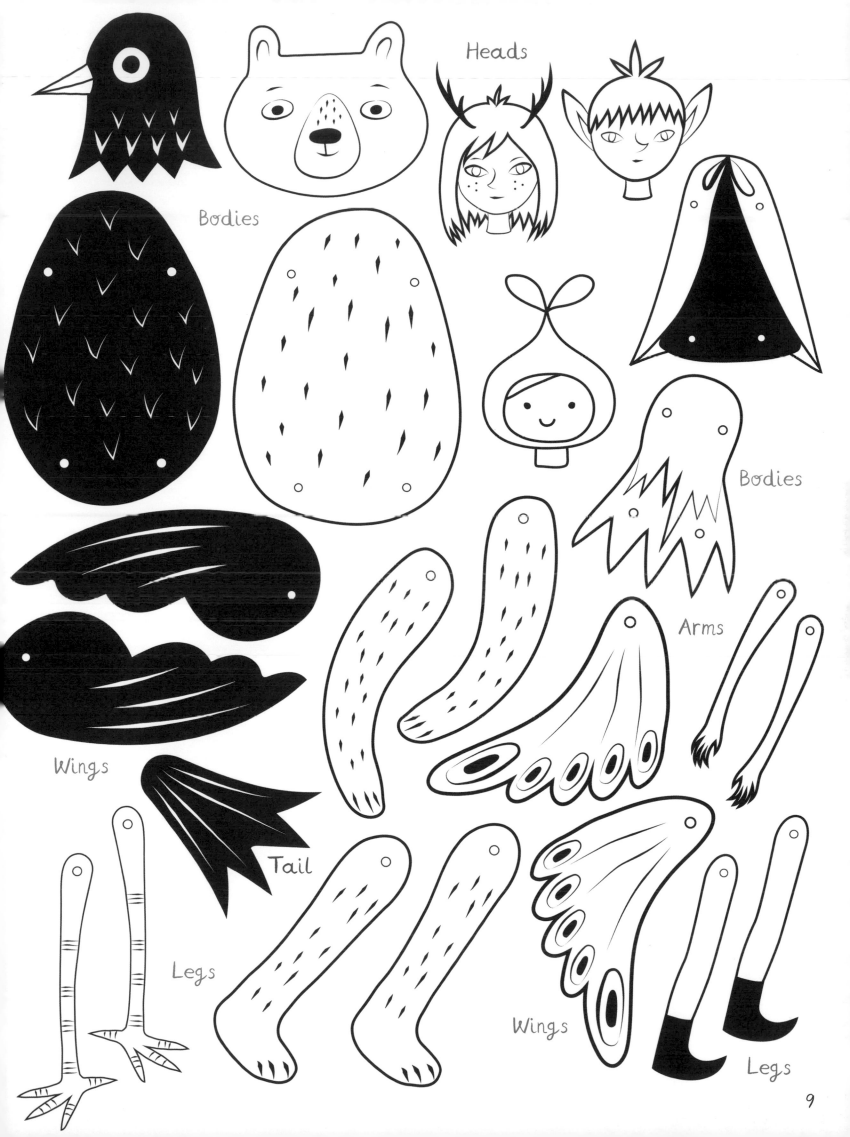

Heads

Bodies

Bodies

Arms

Wings

Tail

Legs

Wings

Legs

9

Treasure trails

Can you help the woodfolk go the correct way through the maze by following the sequence of symbols for each character? Avoid the spiders, and do not go in the water.

Color in all the characters to make them come to life.

How many acorns can you spot?

The forest spirit

This forest spirit is not visible to the human eye. It has a great magical power, which protects the whole woodland, helping to keep it a secret place. Connect the dotted lines to reveal what the spirit looks like.

The collectors

Can you help figure out who has collected the most items and who has collected the fewest?

$5 + 5 =$

$9 + 6 =$

$15 + 10 - 2 =$

$22 - 6 + 2 =$

$5 + 8 - 2 =$

$6 + 5 - 4 + 1 =$

$18 - 5 =$

```
0  1  2  3  4  5  6  7  8  9  10  11  12  13  14  15  16  17  18  19  20  21  22  23  24  25  26
```

This number line can help you add or subtract numbers. Point at the numbers as you solve the problem, moving along the line forward for adding and backward for subtracting. The number that you end on should be the correct answer.

For example: $2 + 2 + 3 - 1 = 6$

```
            2   +2      +3
                              -1
   0  1  2  3  4  5 (6) 7  8  9  10  11
```

SECRET
language

Create your very own secret language that only you can understand. You can share it with a friend by writing them a coded letter. Don't forget to give them the key so that they can translate it. A simple code is to write backward, for example, UOY ERA WOH? is HOW ARE YOU?

The woodfolk have their own secret language called Pigpen. They have left you a message at the bottom of the page to translate using this code:

A	B	C
D	E	F
G	H	I

J.	K.	L.
M.	N.	O.
P.	Q.	R.

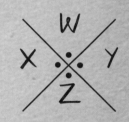

Use the lines and dots surrounding a letter, for example:

H O W   A R E   Y O U ?

⊓⌐∨ ⌐⌐□ <⊏< ?

FACT
The Pigpen code is very old. The name Pigpen comes from the shapes around each letter, which are like little houses or pigpens for them to live in.

Can you translate this coded message from the woodfolk?

⊓⌐∟∟⌐,
>⊓⌐⌐ ⌐∨ ⌐ ⊓⌐⌐⊐⊐⊓.
⊐∪∨∨⌐⊓⊓ ⊏⌐ ⊓⌐⊓⊓ 18
>⊏ ⊓⌐∟⊓ ∨⊏∟∧⊓ >⊓⊓
⊓<∧∧∟⊏.
⊓⊏⊏⊐ ∟<∟⊔ ∟⌐⊏⊐
>⊓⊓ ∨⊏⊏⊐⊐⊏∟⊔

Send a SECRET letter to a friend

Receiving letters and gifts is always a fun experience. Why not send a tiny box to a friend, with a secret coded message inside?

YOU WILL NEED

* Tiny box, e.g. a matchbox
* Scissors
* Piece of paper and a pen
* Address sticker from the middle of the book

1. Write your secret message onto a piece of paper using the Pigpen code (see opposite page) or your own version. Don't forget to include a key so that your friend can figure it out. Try using tiny handwriting (sometimes it helps to write in capital letters to make it easier to read).

2. Fold the letter up, and pop it inside the box. Stick on the address label and write on your friend's address. Use a piece of tape to seal the box shut. Either hand it directly to your friend or deliver it to their mail box.

Use tiny handwriting but make sure your friend can read it!

Fold the letter up as small as you can.

Find a tiny box that the address label fits on.

Seal the box shut with tape or a sticker.

Deliver your box and then wait to see if you receive a reply!

The lost shadows

The woodfolk's shadows have been blown away by a giant troll's enormous sneeze.

Can you match the shadows back up to their correct owner?

Woodfolk TREE House

Whooo Whooo

Decipher the coded message using the key on page 14.

Who lives in this nest? Can you draw them in?

Can you count how many ladders there are?

Help the characters find their homes. Add the woodfolk and furnishings to the rooms using the stickers found in the middle of the book.

19

Draw your own woodland house

Design a
personalized
crest

Mini beasts

Stare at the shapes for a while, then
draw the creature that you see appearing
before your eyes. Some have been done for you.

A → Z

Find an item on the page beginning with each letter of the alphabet. Check them off as you find each one.

Can you find 15 mice?

Missing parts

Draw in the missing parts of these
woodfolk to make them come to life.

24

Who ate the strawberries?

Follow the snail trails to find the culprits.

Fill in the missing numbers in the number sequences.

3 9 15 24 30

2 4 8 12 14 18 22 26 30 36 42 46 50

25

COMPLETE THE BEAR'S FACE

ENERGY
Honey Balls

Easy to make in 10 minutes. No baking!

Gluten-free and yummy!

YOU WILL NEED

Makes approximately 20 balls

1½ cups oats (gluten-free if needed)

½ cup smooth peanut butter

¼ cup honey

¼ cup chopped roasted almonds

(or hazelnuts)

1 tbsp sesame seeds

A pinch of cinnamon

For the outside coating:

3 tbsp sesame seeds or flaked coconut

1. Combine all the ingredients in a large bowl with a wooden spoon.

2. Put about a tablespoon of the mixture into the palm of your hand and roll it into a ball. Repeat until you have used up all the mixture.

3. Put the extra sesame seeds or flaked coconut onto a plate and roll each ball in them until thoroughly coated on the outside.

4. Place the balls onto a plate or in an airtight container and put in the fridge for about an hour, or until you are ready to eat them.

Enjoy your energy-packed snack while on a fun woodland adventure.

The honey keys

The worker bees have dropped all the keys to the queen bee's royal honey palaces. Can you find them all before the other animals do?

How many of each can you spot?

FOXES ◯ BEES ◯

KEYS ◯ BIRDS ◯

The honey palaces

Connect each key to the right honey palace by drawing a line between them.

The
Queen
Bee

Color me in.

Mystery guest

An unexpected guest has messed up the bears' den.
Unscramble the words to match the items in the picture below.

OYNEH _ _ _ _ _   SIHF _ _ _ _

IESERRB _ _ _ _ _ _ _   OSKSC _ _ _ _ _

ESEAVL _ _ _ _ _ _   THSA _ _ _ _

SRUHMSOMO _ _ _ _ _ _ _ _ _   SKBOO _ _ _ _ _

Can you put the bears' socks back into pairs?

Why do bears wear socks?
Because they've got bear feet!

Welcome to the woods, pages 4-5

To:

To:

To:

Mail a secret letter to a friend, page 15

Woodfolk

Woodfolk

Woodfolk

Woodfolk tree house,
pages 18-19

Woodfolk tree house,
pages 18-19

Mystery guest, page 33

Spider math, page 37

Giant troll's weather stickers, page 43

Dress up a unicorn, page 50

Magic dream potion, page 59

Wishing star, page 55

Go to the sticker sheet found in the middle of the book to see
who the mystery guest is and add them to the scene.

Woodland birds

How many birds are there in total? _____

How many nests can you see? _____

Which early bird got the worm?

How many birds are flying? _____

How many crowns can you see? _____

FACT
Hummingbirds are the only birds that can fly backward. The bee hummingbird is the world's smallest bird at just 2in long.

Make suet ball treats for birds to eat:

Melt a pack of lard or suet in a pan over a low heat (with the help of an adult). Mix in a handful of oats, raisins, and bird seed. Then comes the sticky part: with your hands, mold the mixture into tangerine-sized balls and put into a container. Place in the fridge to set. Once set, put the balls into a bird feeder and hang outside. Now watch from a distance to see the little birds arrive.

Complete all the problems to stop the woodfolk from getting stuck in the sticky cobwebs.

×2 web:
14 16 18
12   20
10   2
        4
8   6 4

Look at the instruction in the middle of the web and work around in a circle doing each problem. One has been done for you in each web.

÷2 web:
3
6 4 2
8   20
÷2   18
10   16
12 14

+4 web:
5
1 2
10   3
9 +4 4
8   5
7 6

SPIDER math

Complete the number sequences in the spider's legs to make him dance

45 27 9

24 8

7

21

6

18

30

5 15

4 12 35

20

3 6

2 60

15

10 44

27

How many legs do spiders have? ⚪

Can you give the spider some shoes to wear by putting stickers on his feet? Find them on the sticker sheets in the middle of the book.

Create your very own *magical*
character
for a story

To write a great story, you need to make your characters real and believable so that they come to life. When you become totally immersed in the story, the MAGIC happens and you actually become your character. Fill in the list below to discover more about your new friend.

Your character's name:

KEY CHARACTERISTICS

> Male/female/it?

> How old is it?

> What does it like to eat?

> How big/tall/small is it?

> How is it feeling? (e.g. happy, sad, scared, or lonely)

> What is its goal?

> Where does it live?

> What is its voice like? (try sounding it out loud)

> Who else is in its family?

> What is it good at?

> What is its favorite color?

> What is its magical power?

> Who is its best friend?

> How does it look? (e.g. hairy, feathery, super-fluffy)

Draw your character here

Use your imagination

Roll a story

Roll a dice once for each of the categories in the table, picking the plot detail with the corresponding number. Use your imagination to fill in the rest of the story on the opposite page, giving it a beginning, middle, and end.

Dice number	Character you meet	Place	Action	Problem
●	Mini troll	In a queen bee's honey palace	Grows wings and flies	Magic feather is lost
●●	Sprite	In a bear's dark cave on a mountainside	Jumps up really high	Needs to get a message to the queen
●●●	Hungry bear	A home inside a tree trunk	Can run super fast	Gets caught in a trap
●●●●	Flying squirrel	In a bird's nest	Falls down a giant hole	Needs to rescue their best friend
●●●●●	Tree monster	Underground in a rabbit's warren	Invisible for a few minutes	Gets lost in the woods
●●●●●●	Baby dragon	In a secret woodland, on a sunny morning	Eats a dragon fruit and grows really tall	Finds a locked treasure box

Write down your story

Your main character from pages 38-39:

Character you meet:

Place:

Action:

Problem:

You create the solution/end:

Title: _____

Beginning:

Middle:

End:

Giant trolls
hidden folk

What is this troll thinking about?

Size of a child

What would you say to a giant troll?

Side view

Color in the troll.

Some hills and mountains in the secret woodland are actually giant trolls, fast asleep. They don't like to be disturbed.

42

Bird's-eye view

Imagine you are riding on a swallow's back high up in the sky.
How many giant trolls can you spot hiding in the landscape?
Add some weather stickers from the middle of the book to the sky.

FACT

Many years ago, Scandinavian people believed that trolls
had power over everything, including the weather. These
ancient myths tell of trolls that were frightened of lightning
strikes and that turned to stone when exposed to sunlight.
In Norway, the giant trolls were called
"huldrefolk" (hidden folk).

Mini trolls

Troll folk are usually disguised with leaf and petal-like shapes to help hide themselves amongst the woodland landscape.

Can you give these mini trolls names and write or draw what you think some of them are thinking and talking about?

Spot the difference

There are 8 differences to find between these mini trolls.

Which three mini trolls are exactly the same?

The Bird King

Can you help the Bird King read the message from the birds at the bottom of the page? The birds have dropped some of the letters in the woods. Find and unscramble them to fill in the missing words.

```
F L Y I N G
U W V A S Z
A O E E R T
D R F G E T
F M D D H S
S S K K T E
G E I A A N
E N E L E S
G Z P D F B
K F R M S N
```

Can you find these words?

king   feathers
tree   nest
beak   flying
seeds   worms

YOUR GOLD _ _ _ _ WILL BE READY AT _ O'CLOCK.

FIND IT AT THE TOP OF THE TALL _ _ _ _ TREE.

46

Dress up a woodfolk tree

Use the stickers in the middle of the book to DRESS UP the woodfolk tree.

What is your favorite type of tree?

What is your favorite fruit?

What fruit rhymes with bear?

WE ♥ trees

Trees are the GREEN LUNGS of our planet.

Trees are amazing! They grow fruit, nuts, and spices, and, most importantly, they are the lungs of our planet, which help us breathe. Be kind to trees; we cannot live without them.

Summer
tree

Animals like to store their nuts underground for the cold winter months.

FACT
No two snowflakes are exactly the same. Their forms have almost infinite possibilities.

Please put out suet balls to help the birds during the cold winter months (see recipe on page 35).

Sometimes squirrels forget where they have hidden their nuts. Can you help find them all? How many can you find in total?

Winter
tree

Underground animals are fast asleep hibernating in their burrows.

Dress up a unicorn

Use the stickers from the middle of the book, or draw your own accessories, to dress up the unicorn.

50

How to draw a unicorn

Using a pencil, follow the shapes in the correct sequence, drawing a soft faint line. Go over with markers or pencils to create the final stage.

How to draw a five-pointed star

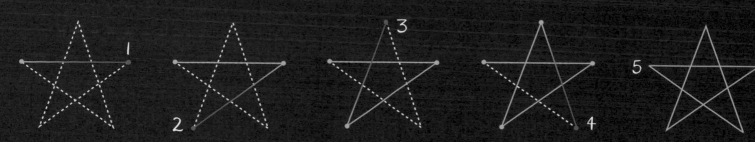

Try drawing this in one sequence without lifting your marker or pencil off the paper.

Mountain yeti

FACT

Did you know that the yeti originates from China? For centuries, people living near the Shennongjia forest have believed that the yeti or "wild man" lives nearby. This tall and hairy creature has been spotted hundreds of times around the mountains and forests, but no one has been able to prove it exists.

Search for the words that appear in the list

Q	S	S	C	I	L	F	R	T
W	W	X	H	A	J	E	Q	W
F	S	B	I	R	D	S	N	G
E	L	N	N	P	T	V	I	S
T	U	V	A	C	R	T	A	D
O	Q	N	J	K	E	I	L	S
E	D	K	H	Y	E	O	V	C
A	K	H	O	U	S	E	R	F

China
Birds
Red panda
Snake
Trees
House
Yeti

Who's been up to my house?

Whose footsteps lead up to the yeti's house?

53

How to draw a bird

Using a pencil, follow the shapes in the correct sequence, drawing a soft, faint line. Color in with colored markers or pencils to create the final stage.

1
2
3
4
5

Try drawing a bird here.

Make a wishing star

YOU WILL NEED
----

* Letter-sized sheet of paper
* Letter-sized sheet of tracing paper
* Pencil & pen
* Ruler
* Scissors
* Sticker to seal the star (found in the middle of the book)

1. Trace the five-pointed star below onto paper or follow the instructions for drawing one on page 51.

2. Cut out the star with scissors.

3. Write a wish on each of the five points and draw them in the center.

4. Fold in all the points where the dotted lines are.

5. Get the wishing star sticker from the middle of the book to seal it closed.

6. Place your special star under your pillow to make your wishes come true.

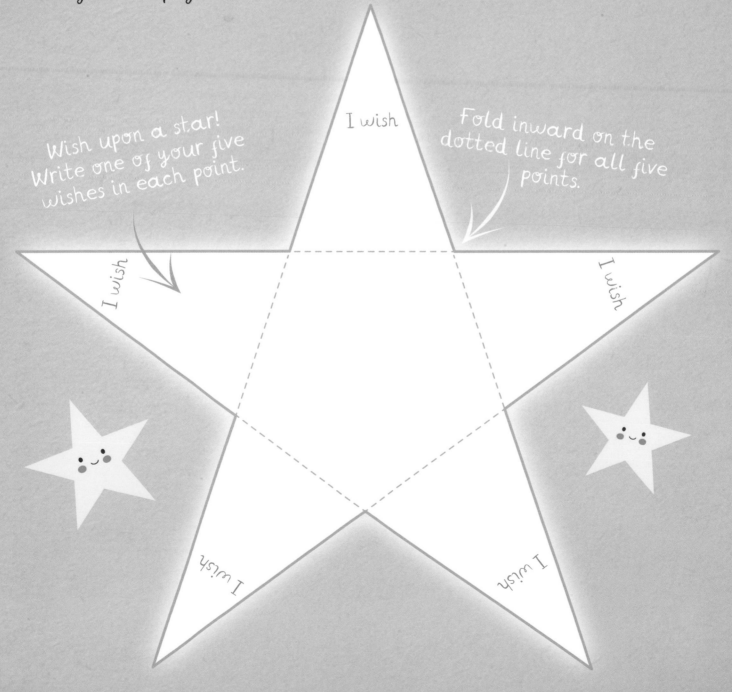

Wish upon a star! Write one of your five wishes in each point.

Fold inward on the dotted line for all five points.

I wish

I wish

I wish

I wish

I wish

Sweet dreams mobile

Create a mobile to hang in your bedroom to give you sweet dreams.

YOU WILL NEED
- - - - - - - - - - - - - -
* Letter-sized sheet of card stock and scissors
* Colored markers or pencils
* Colorful string
* Large sewing needle
* Decorations e.g. beads, shiny stickers, mini pompoms
* Glue

1. Draw and cut out a cloud shape on the card stock.

2. With adult assistance, make a hole with the sewing needle at the top of the cloud and a row of four along the bottom. Loop some string through the top hole for hanging up and add some dangling strings through the bottom holes.

3. Draw your favorite things on the front and back of the cloud-shaped card stock, or add some stickers found in the middle of the book.

4. Add some sparkle and magic by attaching beads, mini pompoms, or cut-out card shapes and stick onto the pieces of string at the bottom, like raindrops.

5. Hang the mobile near your bed to give you lovely sweet dreams.

Draw or add stickers of your favorite things that make you happy.

Add beads, mini pompoms, or cut-out shapes to the strings.

With your sewing needle and string, thread on the mini pompoms.

Flying dreams

If you could fly, what would your wings look like? Draw yourself flying here using colored pencils. White colored pencil and metallic pencils or markers work well on dark colors.

Dream time

This is a little fairy who looks after dreams. Each child has a different dream fairy (just like the tooth fairy). Their job is to carefully mix up a magic potion by selecting ingredients from the secret woodland, such as happy seeds, sparkles, and fluff from the clouds. They are mixed together in a special bottle then sprinkled onto your pillow for lovely sweet dreams.

Your dream fairy is called:

_____

Color in the dream fairy and give it a name to make it yours.

Magic dream potion

Create your own magic dream potion.
Add stickers from the middle of the
book or draw your own ingredients.

What kind of sweet
dreams will it
give you?

Can you remember the last dream you had? Write about it here:

The night sky

Connect the dotted lines to see the star constellations over the secret woodland. White colored pencil and metallic markers or pencils work best on dark colors.

Can you count how many stars there are in total?

Can you color in the magical trail?

Mother Nature likes to work her magic at night while most creatures are sleeping. She leaves a beautiful trail in the sky called the Northern Lights.

FACT
The Northern Lights are known as the aurora borealis. The name aurora comes from the Latin word for sunrise or the Roman goddess of dawn.

At night, the woodfolk carry
night lights to find their way
around the secret woodland.
Can you color in some of the
characters and plants to make
them come to life?

The night time

Answers

Page 7: height order = 5, 4, 3, 2, 1, 7, 6. Pages 10–11: 10 acorns. Page 13: 5 + 5 = 10, 9 + 6 = 15, 22 - 6 + 2 = 18, 5 + 8 - 2 = 11, 15 + 10 - 2 = 23 (most), 18 - 5 = 13, 6 + 5 - 4 + 1 = 8 (fewest). Page 14: Secret message = Hello, there is a hidden message on page 18 to help you solve the puzzle. Good luck from the woodfolk. Pages 18–19: 8 ladders; secret message = Bear has lost his hat, can you find it? Pages 22–23: A = ants, acorn, apple; B = bear, bells, birds, bat, butterfly, blossom, bunting, bows, bush; C = crown, cave, chick, clover, cricket, crows, cheese; D = drum, daisies; E = eggs, eyes, eggshell; F = flag, fox, four-leaf clover, flower; G = grass; H = hedgehog; I = ice-cream, insects; J = jar, jelly; K = kite; L = leaves, ladybug, letters; M = mountains, moths, music, mice, meadow, maracas; N = nest, notes; O = owls; P = parachute, panda; Q = queen ant; R = rabbit, raindrops, raccoon; S = strawberry, spider, snail, sky, stars, string; T = triangle, trees, trumpet, teepee, tortoise; U = umbrella; V = violin; W = water, web, wings, woodland; X = xylophone; Y = yeti; Z = zebra. Page 25: sequence 1 = 3, 6, 9, 12, 15, 18, 21, 24, 27, 30; sequence 2 = 2, 4, 6, 8, 10, 12, 14, 16, 18, 20, 22, 24, 26, 28, 30, 32, 34, 36, 38, 40, 42, 44, 46, 48, 50. Pages 28–29: 6 foxes, 4 bees, 13 keys, 7 birds. Page 32: unscrambled words = honey, berries, leaves, fish, mushrooms, socks, blanket, pillow, hats, books. Pages 34–35: 55 birds, 4 nests, bird with worm is blackbird on top left branch, 5 flying birds, 3 crowns. Page 36: (clockwise from given answer) top web = 8, 12, 16, 20, 24, 28, 32, 36, 40; middle web = 2, 1, 10, 9, 8, 7, 6, 5, 4; bottom web = 6, 7, 8, 9, 10, 11, 12, 13, 14. Page 37: number sequences in spider's legs clockwise starting from top right: 5, 10, 15, 20, 25, 30, 35, 40, 45, 50, 55, 60, 65, 70; 4, 8, 12, 16, 20, 24, 28, 32, 36, 40, 44, 48; 3, 6, 9, 12, 15, 18, 21, 24, 27, 30; 2, 4, 6, 8, 10, 12, 14, 16, 18, 20; 6, 12, 18, 24, 30, 36, 42, 48, 54, 60; 7, 14, 21, 28, 35, 42, 49, 56, 63, 70; 8, 16, 24, 32, 40, 48, 56, 64, 72, 80, 88, 96; 9, 18, 27, 36, 45, 54, 63, 72, 81, 90, 99, 108, 117, 126; spider has 8 legs. Page 43: 8 giant trolls hidden. Page 46: hidden message = Your gold nest will be ready at 8 o'clock. Find it at the top of the tall blue tree. (The number 8 is hidden in the bird's crown.) Page 48–49: 28 nuts hidden. Page 53: the bird. Page 60–61: 42 stars.

For my beautiful girls, Lilly & Eva

A big thank you to my lovely husband, my parents and my in-laws for looking after the kids during the holidays and for all your loving support. I love you.

And, a huge Jeg Elsker Dig to all my Danish relatives.

First published 2019 by Button Books, an imprint of Guild of Master Craftsman Publications Ltd Castle Place, 166 High Street, Lewes, East Sussex BN7 1XU.
Text © Mia Underwood, 2019. Copyright in the Work © GMC Publications Ltd, 2019. Illustrations © Mia Underwood, 2019. ISBN 978 1 78708 027 0. Distributed by Publishers Group West in the United States. All rights reserved. Reprinted 2020, 2023. The right of Mia Underwood to be identified as the author of this work has been asserted in accordance with the Copyright, Designs, and Patents Act 1988, sections 77 and 78. No part of this publication may be reproduced, stored in a retrieval system, or transmitted in any form or by any means without the prior permission of the publisher and copyright owner. This book is sold subject to the condition that all designs are copyright and are not for commercial reproduction without the permission of the designer and copyright owner. While every effort has been made to obtain permission from the copyright holders for all material used in this book, the publishers will be pleased to hear from anyone who has not been appropriately acknowledged and to make the correction in future reprints. The publishers and author can accept no legal responsibility for any consequences arising from the application of information, advice, or instructions given in this publication. A catalog record for this book is available from the British Library.
Publisher: Jonathan Bailey; Production: Jim Bulley, Jo Pallet; Senior Project Editor: Virginia Brehaut; Managing Art Editor: Gilda Pacitti. Color origination by GMC Reprographics. Printed and bound in China.
Warning! Choking hazard - small parts. Not suitable for children under 3 years.

For more information on Button Books, contact:
GMC Publications Ltd Castle Place, 166 High Street, Lewes, East Sussex, BN7 1XU, United Kingdom
Tel: +44 (0)1273 488005   www.buttonbooks.co.uk